Journey to the Moons

Poems about the different moons in the galaxy.

Journey to the Moons

Poems about the different moons in the galaxy.

AALIYA ASHFAQ

Bigfoot Publications
Because, there's a writer in everyone.

Journey to the Moons
Author : Aaliya Ashfaq

First Published by
Bigfoot06 Publications (OPC) Pvt. Ltd.
1st floor, BSR Building near Vishal Mega Mart,
Daultabad Flyover, Laxman Vihar Phase 3,
Gurugram, Haryana (122001)
Website: www.bigfootpublications.in
Email: info@bigfootpublications.in

First Edition : October, 2023

ISBN Print Book - 978-81-19512-30-0

Printed in India

Acknowledgement

I am deeply grateful to my family, my friends and colleagues. Thank you for lending an ear, offering insights, and reminding me to keep pushing forward.

To the people I love, who have stayed with me throughout the good and bad experiences.

To the dedicated team at Bigfoot Publications, your support in bringing this project to life has been exceptional.

To my reader, I thank you for accompanying me as we travel to the various moons of our universe while still being on Earth. I hope you find your favorite moon.

About the moon

The sapphire moon engulfs every dweller who visions it. What if I told you that the moons of other planets had songs to sing and stories to tell?

Content

I.

Moons of Mars

Phobos

If you were to ask me for advice,

I would tell you to never make anyone the center of your universe.

It doesn't exist. And even if it did, We are all very far away.

They might become your center, but all you will do is spin,

Until one day, uncontrollably, you will drift,

And once you stray away from your orbit, you will spin aimlessly.

Deimos

I made friends and foes,
We had our highs and lows.
I do not regret what I lost,
I do not exclaim over what I gained.
You see, I have accepted the universe for everything it is.
Because I tried fighting once,
And I failed.
But don't try to be me.
If you feel that going against the universe is your last shot,
Barge in with everything.
Break barriers and blow up everything.
Don't settle like me.

II.

Moons of Jupiter

Callisto

We sat gazing at the sky on a full moon night,
Still staring at the sky he asked,
What's your favorite thing out there?
'Callisto' I said followed by a smile.
Puzzled he asked why?
The Galilean moon, a moon of Jupiter among its four,
She is the most cratered thing in our universe.
But, every time a crater forms it freezes,
It forms huge crystals of ice.
These ice crystals never melt,
And hence reflect the sun with all they have.
I wish I could be like that.
Damaged, yet so beautiful.
Hit with almost everything in this universe,
She still revolves with her wounds.
Freezes everything that causes it,
And shines brighter than before.
I wish we could see it from here, I told him.
I already am he said, looking at me intently.

Io

I brew volcanoes deadlier than the ones you've seen.
For sometimes we bottle up
Too much of what should be released.
As I erupt and reshape everything around me,
I wish I had been open to articulating
Those thousand endless possibilities.

Elara

Mysteriously, we revolve,
All you can do is make assumptions from afar.
But the real challenge is getting to know me,
Studying my history,
Observing the aftermath of storms
That took place billions of years ago.
You say the distance is too far to cross,
That perhaps observing me is the best.
What if I told you everything you know about me
Is far from what you should know?
But maybe someday, when you get to me,
You shall understand the false presumptions.
For once, maybe you will know what I can be.

Sinope

Inconsistencies are like wishful thinking,

Contradictory, yet so necessary.

I want someone to question unanswered questions,

I want them to discover more about the hidden world.

I know it's easy to make assumptions from afar,

But there is beauty in traversing the distance.

Ask an astronaut how they felt

When they saw everything from space.

I appreciate the existence of unexplainable events and encounters.

One such moment was when we first met.

Ganymede

The largest of its kind,

Do not mistake it to be blind.

The moon of a giant is its attribute,

But among other treasuries, frost is what it loots.

Gallant as always, Ganymede stayed upright.

But tell me, how do you determine courage?

How do you keep your heart open,

To the one set on destroying it?

Shall I tell you why his heart is made of metal?

For he never saw love

As delicate as a petal.

"Don't despise Ganymede," I tell him,

For he belongs to the giants.

A big heart may suffer a great deal,

But a cold one does not feel.

"Why turn a heart to metal?" he asked.

Meteorites may appear as shining stars from afar,

How would you discern their intentions?

Europa

The smallest among the four, a vessel of hope.
Life in the unknown, harboring without sight.
What do you know about the secrets she hides?
What could you grasp of the beings she bore?

Voyagers set out to seek her,
She tells them she bears no gifts.
As an open mirror, she stands,
Witnessing the miracles of the defiant.

She held a labyrinth within her,
But who told you it would lead to gold?
Foretold, you were warned,
As she carries the hidden world,
And she might open up to you
If truth is what you seek.

Carme

We all hold broken pieces
Somehow mine float.
Like a moon, when a part of me breaks,
It drifts through the universe.
How beautiful that is,
Everything witnesses what broke me,
You could piece it back into me like a jigsaw puzzle.
But I want you to see it,
I've let go of something that no longer holds value;
You can too.

Iocaste

Beams of light traverse the universe,
Hitting surfaces and bouncing everywhere.
I sent one to you,
But it got lost en route.
I think about the million things that are lost in space,
Even we are lost in solace.
Dreams and wishes, stars and kisses,
All of them find themselves lost in some corner,
But today I will send you another ray of light.
I'm uncertain about when or whether it will reach you,
But if it does,
You'll know
That someone out there still loves you.

Cyllene

Do you know we echo?

We sing, shout, and scream.

Yet, our space is a vacuum, So, it dissipates.

Your world isn't.

So, scream, shout, and roar.

Make your voice heard.

There will be people attempting to stifle it,

Trying to create a void,

But defy the space,

And scream until their ears bleed.

Amalthea

Can all of this be a hoax?
You, me and our dreams.
Have you ever felt so lost,
That you never want to be found again?
My secret hums and teary eyes,
I wish I knew in your world time flies.
How do you humans deal with pain?
How do you let go off someone so easily?
Look at us moons,
With a million things wanting to destroy us,
We can't fathom about leaving our planets.
Yet you find comfort with someone else,
When your heart belongs somewhere else.

Eupheme

They say that we are a small part of this big universe,
But, I'd like to think we are more than that.
If everyone felt that the universe wouldn't be the same,
Without their existence,
Don't you think they would stop trying,
To fit in a world that was not a maze?
Do you think the other creatures of your world,
Feel that they don't belong here?
With your fast-moving structures, they still find new homes,
And you feel you don't belong somewhere.
You try to create homes within people,
People who change within seconds.
I know it's harsh,
But people are fickle.
They change minds, words and feelings within no time.

Sponde

Ponds of thoughts fell as tears,

Do heart breaks happen only here or even far away?

How should I tell you it is all just the same,

We are meant to fall and get up again.

You ask me how many times till I break?

I tell you till you're strong enough to love yourself without pain.

Himalia

Blissful memories,

Happy faces, happier times.

If I knew it was meant to repeat like a cycle,

Maybe I would have been wise.

Erinome

Glittering facades, Shimmering vibes.
How do you trust something,
Which was designed to lie.
As I lie awake,
Wondering how could I be so blind.
You pierced what was left of me,
And left me to die.

Arche

Taken for granted is such a funny phrase
Only if I could explain the technicality.
You see it is a negligent affirmation.
A complete paradox.
Maybe our love was such.
There were great possibilities
As well as diminishing chances.
Only if I knew that relationships
Could be this complicated.

Helike

If you refer to someone as your moon,
Prepare yourself to not see them,
On certain concealed days.
Accept that on occasions,
they will be at their farthest,
And on some days,
they might even vanish.
Yet, they will never truly abandon your side,
So, reconsider your choice,
Before you make someone as your moon.

Carpo

I like how you have prioritized things in your world,
Yet, how do you set apart things that cannot be compared?
If I gave you choice to make,
Would you choose the profit?
Or would you choose yourself?
Strange how when we mention priorities,
We think about everyone,
Except for ourselves.

Metis

The moon in your world may be bright,
But not every moon.
As we move far away from the sun,
We're just plainly revolving around our planets.
But that does not stop us from being called a moon.
So why do you stop?
Just because you are not shining today.

Ananke

Parallel universes are confusing.
You tell me there is a possibility
Of a world where everything is perfect.
But there is also a chance
That a grim, wicked world prospers
Where every worst nightmare is set to occur.
I shall always choose the present one,
For I would not want the others,
Not because they are fantasies,
Neither because they are possible.
But would you want to live in a world
Where nothing is governed by faith?
Don't wish for something perfect,
When you were given what you needed.

Themisto

They asked me what are the warning signs in a universe that is quiet,
I told them, it's the eyes.
The eyes tell you what you need to know,
They show you what you don't want to know.
But, the silly heart takes no heed.
It learns only through experience,
And falters without any lead.
Look back at everything that you lost,
The warning signs were there,
Loud and clear,
For nature is designed that way.
Storms announce themselves,
For you were a storm too.
Brewing quietly,
I only took notice of you,
When you became a cyclone,
Churning with hate and destruction.
You left me in havoc,
Dead and reeling for hope.
But it was my fault,
After all the rain was the warning sign,
Which I blissfully ignored.

Pasiphae

Shall I tell you about supernova?
Massive explosions,
Blinding lights,
Piercing depositions,
Unheard plights.
Spectrum of colors,
Powerful vibrations.
Fragments become smaller,
Vision becomes brighter.
For a star to be born,
The dwarf had to collapse.
But the leftover nebula gave meaning.
After all, releasing what you hold,
Leads to both,
Destruction and birth rigid as the foreteller's oath.

Adrastea

Rereading my old chapters,
I come across lines,
Where my present self questions,
Why did you stay quiet?
How do I tell myself,
That in that moment,
I lit myself on fire.
But my screams were not heard,
My teary eyes blurred.
You can tell someone you are in pain,
And have them acknowledge for say.
But at the end of the day,
All one can do is hold themselves.
There are no angels, there are no saviors.
I wish I could save myself,
I wish I could blanket far beyond the sky's reach.
But how could I?
When the protagonist was only a child.

Callirrhoe

To the words I never told you,
To the days I never showed you.
To the letters I never sent you,
To the calls I never made,
To the promised I failed.
To the days I never showed up,
To the nights I never stayed.
To the thoughts I held,
To the times I never helped you.
To all the things we never said to each other.
All along, we knew.

Megaclite

I found you broken,

Completely scattered like a broken asteroid.

Your pieces were magnificent,

Filled with hope and faith.

You looked at yourself like a puzzle,

Unsolvable and questionable.

Absurd yet daunting.

For a minute I considered solving you,

Among the million pieces that lie ahead me.

But you were a brave one,

You told me you weren't broken.

The determined fallen.

You told me you were not solving the puzzle,

Merely rearranging the ruffle.

Kalyke

Your world races with time,

Trying to achieve the prize.

What if I told you,

You were doing everything fine.

Not everything can be received,

Before it's time.

Praxidike

No, the universe does not align to give you what you wish,
Nor does it conspire for coincidences.
Why give credit to a universe that merely exists,
With no predictions or affirmations?
Dear soul, this universe runs on energies.
And as the law states it can neither be created or destroyed,
The unheard prayer is a small energy that you released,
And the universe must honor it.
By either giving you something converted,
Or something diverted.

Aitne

Light and sound travel in our space constantly.
Light makes us see things microscopically,
Sound makes us feel vibrations we never received.
It's all a play between the both,
But I heard it's much more astonishing in your world.
How wonderful it is to see light in someone's eye,
And hear sound in someone's voice.
A treat if they come from the same source.

Lysithea

In the chaos of the gazillion things that float here,
I wish to tell you,
No matter how many realities you receive,
No matter how many dreams you wish for,
No matter how much you fight,
No matter how much you cry.
Among all the stars, suns and moons,
What is meant and written,
Will find you.

Autonoe

We talk about distances in light years,
Long distances but so much to convey.
Maybe that's why moments with you,
Fly by.

Thyone

I didn't know some bonds could be chaotic yet so controlled.

If you were smart you would realize that chaos and control are polarities not meant to interact.

But, you and I were different.

We were a mixture of control and chaos.

Maybe that's why we disintegrated.

Your need to have everything under control and my flare to run with chaos was a perfect recipe for a disaster.

And I thought something was wrong with me for not having things planned as you.

Hermippe

Of all the million opportunities,
Available in this small world.
I pray to the Creator,
That I meet you at the horizon,
Or where ever the world ends.
After all, I diligently followed the path,
Never asking for a wish.
But if I told you about the number of shooting stars,
I came across,
It's you I prayed for without a doubt.

Aitne

Only if you knew about the number of things,
That moved for your heart to exist.
Several stars collided,
And pieces of rubble floated.
The back end is important.
The play cannot work without the run crews,
So for your story to work,
You have to fall and someone has to crash.

Eurydome

To the right people with wrong timing,

Do you get to meet again?

Do you get to do it again?

Do you get the second chance you so badly desired?

Or do you leave it as it is?

I wish there was an answer to this,

I wish there was a perspective to this.

Euanthe

We have various space tunnels that float.
Some carry prayers unheard,
Some carry thoughts unexpressed,
And some carry wishes unfulfilled.
All of these bounce across the tunnel,
Wanting to escape.
So never give up on prayers and dreams,
After all the more energy it receives,
The more likely it will be released.
Never give up on wishes,
After so many revolutions,
I have realized this world is too big for a small wish.
Do not hold things unsaid,
I have seen souls on the other end,
Wishing for one chance to say what they couldn't.

Euporie

What is more dangerous?
A heart that does not beat,
Or a wound that does not bleed? I would say,
It is a soul that does not feel.

Orthosie

To feel heat, you must lightly graze the sun.
To feel wet, you must let the rain touch your face.
To feel power, you must crush someone's heart,
And to feel peace you must let go off a piece.
After all, struggle demands to be felt.

Pasithee

I look at Earth and I see countless planes,
Constantly flying in the quiet of the sky.
You made travel easy on your planet,
I travel ages and distances just to see a glimpse of my love,
How fortunate you are to meet your loved ones,
Within a matter of few hours,
Appreciate moments, for if you were me,
Your heart would wither and cry just to see them smile.

Hegemone

To everyone who runs,
From obstacles, emotions and people.
I wish to tell you,
That you weren't being chased,
There was love you deserved.
Love which was not given,
Love which was taken,
Till you were left with fear.
I stand here to tell you,
This world is circular.
You will end up where you started.

Mneme

Things between the lines,
Draw pictures that are intertwined.
Why make an undecided future,
Crawl through the spaces of unknown?
Why complicate words,
When you already know,
The things that you should say,
But you rather stay safe.
Focused conversations,
Blurry intentions,
You played with lines,
Until I plucked you out like a vine.

Aoede

I saw a burning house,
With no place to hide, they tried to run.
With no one to call they screamed.
The passerby watched,
They marveled at the situation,
But it was not their house.
The firetruck cruised with speed,
It was not what they needed.
Tears fell like a river,
As they braced themselves.
The house that sheltered them,
Pierced them once again.
Did I forget to mention,
There was no fire to begin with.

Thelxinoe

A love like parallel lines,
With so much common,
We were never meant to meet.
But I wish there was a universe out there,
Where we cross paths.

Kallichore

To the little child that walked on knives,
And sheltered herself from thieving eyes.
I wish for a universe,
Where you float on clouds of love,
Fly with hearts of gold.

Chaldene

Everything that happens outside is immense.

Asteriods crashing,

Stars burning,

Planets deflecting,

Meteorites lighting,

Comets flying.

Everything is immense.

Maybe that's why

Souls meeting is also immense.

Heightened sense,

Promises of suspense.

Yes, that's why it is so intense.

Dia

People always say what they think is the best for you.
Yes, I know, who would advise you anything that would harm you?
I wish I hadn't listened to them.
They told me about a world,
That ceased to exist.
I entered a new world,
With old experiences.
Only to fall harder, only to falter in pain.

III.

Moons of Saturn

Tethys

Shall I not tell you about how we are struck time and again,
These craters might look beautiful to you,
But oh how painful they were.
You find comfort when wounded,
But in this vast universe,
All we do is rotate.
They tell us scars distinguish us from the rest,
Someone tell them next time might be our last test.
For another blow, I might drift away.
And away from the rings, I might never find place.
We hear echoes of them,
Racing to hit us again.
Sometimes all they leave are craters but sometimes they perish.
For I wish I was the sun,
They would burn from far ahead,
But I am only a moon, how would I suffice?

Pandora

In a land far away,
I chose to stay,
Small and confined, space is full of lies.
What is the point of being gifted?
Is it being proud or is it being humble?
I was gifted an epiphany,
For all those who came to seek Saturn would see me.
The Golden Age, where I was better than the others,
But if you ask me who is the biggest destroyer,
Time is who I would point at.
Time is nasty as it is easy to be forgotten,
Easy to lose track and easy to perish.
How many friends I lost, just because time didn't hold.
My acquaintances sank in this null void of time,
Rust is not what destroys metal
But merely the time it was left unattended.
So I plead,
For if you have forgotten a friend or foe,
Destruction never knocks on the door.
Amend what time broke,
An ode to everything broken.

Janus

Open doorways lead to new beginnings,
Moving away from you,
Would be a new beginning.
How wrong was I to bring in old baggage,
It haunted me forever
That I couldn't get rid of it. I look into the portal,
The future and past are crystal clear,
If only I had been warned about the errors
I was going to create,
A different course is what I would have set
I stand before a gate,
Unknown to the secrets behind it,
If I knew you would have changed my life this way,
Your key is what I would have thrown away.
Nevertheless, I stand before a new door,
Scared that I don't forgo,
Memories can be tainted,
Only if the universe had given me a sign,
Your knock, I should have aborted.
I swing these gates open,
With a hope that I don't make the same mistakes,
I wish you were a distant dream,
A dream that I could forget.

Telesto

Out of every concept you created,
Infinity is my favorite.
Your world quantified everything,
Seasons, years and months,
Days, time and seconds.
You live a numbered life,
But infinity engulfs all might.
There is an infinite space out here,
And I love to think that the heart is infinite,
If ever asked how much you love someone,
Please say 'infinite'
Do not say you love them as much as the moon
Because there is a distance beyond that.
Do not tell them you love them as much as the universe,
Another might exist.
Do not tell them as much as the biggest star,
There are stars we don't even know about.
But tell them you love them to infinity,
As it is beyond all.
You will love them infinitely in this universe
And the next.

Titan

I have layers of ice as I
Defend myself against cruelty.
Voyager you seek to inhabit me,
You peek through your glass,
To see the water gush out of me.
But, as I follow the rings,
I tell, your world cannot exist in mine.
Voyager, you and I are different
In this vast universe we seek for answers,
And I am not the answer you seek.
We tend to think that compromise is a solution,
Why would you travel so far for
Something available in abundance.
Why would you search depths for love,
While you hold it within yourself?
Discovery is beautiful
But not at the cost of destruction.
We took years to shape,
So don't tell me course of things will change.
For in your world, nothing is stagnant.
Don't abandon what is yours,
In the path of finding void.

Skoll

I'd cross galaxies for you,
Fight through the million things that hit me too.
I'd jump across planets and fly through the debris,
Only to see a glimpse of you.

Iapetus

We all aimlessly float around.
You and I, we don't know where we are headed.
You believe in a greater good,
Far beyond this beautiful world,
But the reason why you'll never see the peak,
Is because you destroyed what you had.

How do I tell you that pushing away from things that make you feel,
Is not how you heal?
How should I ask you to embrace and let go of things with grace?
I am not afraid to break again.
Not everyone is seeking to cause destruction.

But I shall tread carefully, For what comes next.

Bestla

I know the others talk about the constant hits and misses,
They like to tell you how they escaped.
But I shall tell you about the things they forgot to mention,
I see meteorites move faster than the speed of light,
I see stars in the last stage of supernova,
I see colors you have never seen
And I dream of everything I could be.
You can be a sour moon and complain about
Everything you think is wrong.
Or you can be me and wonder
About what more the world has to offer.

Calypso

I wish we could travel the universe,
I would show you everything light and bright,
We would lose count of the shapes,
We would get lost in the stars.
I'd show you the beauty of us crossing paths.
I'd show you everything around and in between.
Only if you knew about me,
Only if you had chosen me.

Pallene

Everything from far can look astounding yet deceptive,
I thought you were a nebula,
Exploding with different colors.
Only when you engulfed my soul,
I realized you were a black hole.

Rhea

Quests are interesting,

As you wish to seek something impossible.

But you were not a quest,

You were a bequest. Soft and shallow,

Filled with racing thoughts.

I was meant to protect you And keep you safe.

But you felt like a prisoner and escaped.

Now I look at the castle I built for you,

A cage that you assumed.

So many look out for us,

But we never have reasons,

For why we do what we do.

Enceladus

Approvals are the nastiest,
We seek acceptance amongst everything,
While decreasing our worth.
If you find yourself
Seeking approval for yourself,
Find another stay.
You will be consumed like us,
Do you think we were asked?
If we wanted to be a moon or a star.
Do you think every one of us approved?
The names and attributes we were given.
Sometimes the biggest approvals can feel like hinges,
But not calling the shot will make you cringe.
So be wise.

Dione

In this vast universe,
What were the odds of us meeting?
In this diverse universe,
What were the odds of you leaving?
If I knew your presence was going to cause the domino effect
I would have run away.
But I stayed,
Despite falling carelessly, I stuck with you.
Wait was all you told me,
So I waited patiently,
Until I went crazy.
You told me to wait calmly,
So I waited persistently,
Until I fell apart.
You told me to wait pleadingly,
But I said I wouldn't.
If I could ask the ringmaster, why play such a game?
I'd ask the universe to never cross our paths again.

Greip

You do not have to open to me,
You do not have to tell me your darkest secrets.
You cannot find about moons without discovering,
You cannot love without recovering.
Time can be infinite and short at the same time,
So I made up my mind about not hurrying.
Let's learn about each other's scars with patience,
Let us assume, we have all eternity.

Hyperion

Chaos is what I am known for,
For I can't sit still or stay silent
The stars, the trees
All we do is spin.
Through these dark skies,
You wish for a sunrise
But all I want to do is reach the end,
And patience is not my friend.
They ask me why am I in a hurry,
To reach the horizon,
I tell them what has this universe given me?
For what shall I slow down?
I might get lost with the speed I move,
For I am in search of a void.
They tell me circles have no end,
For I am eternally bounded in a loop.
I still hope to escape,
For I want to see this universe too,
Flow into a different galaxy without being fooled.
Mesmerized by the beauty of the rings,
I came too close,
Now all life, I move a path I didn't choose.

IV.

Moons of Neptune

Triton

We lay awake on sleepless nights,
Thoughts haunt us like restless ghosts,
In this wild world,
I lost the meaning of the right
And memories froze like the frost.
If only I was a time turner,
Or maybe on a different planet itself.
Where the time was slower and the moon was bigger,
I'd tell you everything unsaid,
I'd hold you closer.
I'd do everything I said.

Nereid

So near

Yet the distance between us feels like light years.

I wish I hadn't said those things

I wish I could take back everything in a blink.

The fear of losing you is immense,

I cannot wait another lifetime just to feel the same.

But right now I wish I could heal what I broke,

I don't want you to drift, far away.

Naiad

Countless minutes,
Uncountable feelings.
Numerous apologies,
Unnumbered broken pieces.
Boundless relations,
Measureless emotions.
Bottomless emptiness,
Endless suffering.
Indeterminable consequences,
Immeasurable tears.
This was our story,
Simply profound and incomprehensible.

Thalassa

My planet is a beautiful blue,
But blue is complicated.
Blue oceans, blue skies,
Just like those disheartened cerulean eyes.
As much as blue is calm, it is also cold.
Your eyes reflected a sorrow.
Swirling with confusion and hesitation,
I saw my planet in disguise.
So I ask for advice, Is pain so harsh,
That it draws red veins in those eyes?

Despina

As beautiful as this universe is
It is equally painful.
They may describe the beauty of this world
Again and again,
But pain is what I received.
Trying to make a placc in your world,
How many planets and moons did you discard just because
They didn't fit your definition?
For someone else out there,
Who did regard us equally,
I'll tell you, your kind differentiates.
Your own world revolts within it,
For every crime, you place on the minority.
Clearly, you don't wish to say,
Threatened is what you feel.

Galatea

You and I,
We watch the same stars form,
And we watch the same storms.
How blessed I feel
To share my stardust with you,
But in another world,
I wish we were together.

Larissa

Do you know why do we cling on to
Nostalgia so much?
We think that it will be the closest to happiness
We ever received.
Don't try to recreate them,
They won't feel the same.
Just like the gazillion stars that surround me,
Create new ones,
For this world is full of possibilities.

Proteus

Do you believe people can be thunderstorms?
Loud and quick with rage.
Do you believe people can be forests?
A place to get lost easily.
Do you believe people can be a valley of flowers?
Everblooming and filled with constant hope.
Do you believe people can be sunrises?
Blinding to the eye but warmth to the heart.
I hope your belief does not cease,
For all the probabilities,
For all the years I've spent,
I have learned that they can be,
Oceans filled with force,
Mountain built to create course.
Gardens filled with ivies,
Avalanches ready to crumble.
Lesson is what you gain from the fumble.

Halimede

As we watch the sun from far,
We think about the lunar moon.
The closest to the sun,
The brightest among all.
How I wish I could trade places,
Just to feel the warmth,
But I realized that the lunar moon
Suffered equally and silently.
I wonder why you love the moon and squint at the sun,
When the sun is what makes it the moon.
You think the moon illuminates the night,
But where do you think it gets its light?

Psamathe

What is a burden I asked?
They told me it was excess baggage.
I couldn't help but understand how someone could be a burden?
What exactly was it?
Was it the truth or the hope?
Was it the mercy or the anguish?
Was it the memories or the disappointment?
I felt it was harsh of your world to think of someone as load.
Unless, you wanted to carry a bag
Of things you didn't need.
I spent the whole day wondering about this,
Does my planet consider me a burden?
A luggage he can't get rid off?
But then he told me something astonishing.
Your world plays the blame game,
And this game always has a strong name.
After all they need to prove the things done,
Hence they built guilt and burdens.
Not to show gratefulness, But to declare pride.
No one in this world can be a burden, If you feel like one,
You are in the wrong place.

Sao

We are often told to release
Negative energies,
We do not realize the damage
It causes to our peace.
When we let go off all that is dark and cloudy,
We think this form of cleanse is all that we need.
But when withdrawal strikes you,
All questions seem to kill the ease.
Yes, you have to kill things that don't give you peace,
But do realize it comes with a price.
A price you should be willing to pay,
A pain you should bear.
For healing begins with a slight discomfort,
After all it is nature's way.

Laomedeia

How tiny your core is,
A small dot in front of our rock-solid cores.
But the weight in yours is unfathomable.
How do you carry so much,
Love, hate and anguish?
Maybe that's why he made a cage for your core.
If left wild, I wonder the havoc it would cause.

Neso

If you think every moon is round in shape,

You are misinformed.

Some look like sponges

Some look like small asteroids.

If you think being a perfect sphere

Is the qualifying factor for being a moon.

Change your surroundings dear one,

For you are living in a judgmental world.

Moons come in all shapes and sizes.

All colors and features.

Some are bigger than your planet and some will fit in easily.

But moons orbit their planets,

Their features do not stop them from being called a moon.

So don't let anyone tell you,

You can't be you.

Hippocamp

We often crash with a multitude of things,

Sometimes we are lucky to escape,

Most of the time we meet our demise.

And then we leave behind our old identity.

I know that I am still a moon,

But your world would classify me as something else.

So I leave behind a question,

If your loved one woke up and did not remember you,

What would be the first thing you would tell them to bring back their memories?

Would you tell them what you mean to them or would you tell them how you met?

Would you tell them about your journey or would you tell them about the love you held?

Would you struggle to portray your affection or would you bring pictures to relive memories again?

I want to know the answer. I lost my other half.

And I had nothing to show and nothing to say.

I watched them drift away.

I worked hard on drawing a map of the stars,

Showing them the path and scars.

All in vain,

Sometimes you meet people,

And their purpose was only to forget.

V.

Moons of Uranus

Ariel

They say the world is spinning too quickly,
That time is running out of hands.
They say I have a lot to accomplish,
The stepping stones have been switched.
After all we follow a path,
That leads to a destiny of success.
Only if you knew the truth,
Only if you paid attention.
All of us spin around our planets.
We follow a fixed orbit,
We follow the path promised.
We found out we are headed for a collision,
That our galaxy will merge with another.
So I do not know where I would end up,
Or even survive for the best.
So when I tell you,
Following a fixed path has not brought anyone gain,
But again, you are the sole traveler,
Avoid the mistakes that will lead to pain.

Umbriel

We all try to place ourselves in this universe,
Struggling to find meaning,
Hesitating to find heeding.
Unaware of the chain reactions,
Clueless about the great oppression.
As you stand in a crowd of billions,
Trying to understand existence,
We moons pray daily,
To stick by our planets.
As we fear separation,
And we have seen the magnitude of space.
It is nothing compared to your trivial matters,
And yet you ponder of the future,
With no assurance, you will make it today.
So I ask you, is it really worth it?
A mere dot in my eyes,
But there is somewhere else where we all are dots,
Running around just to make sense.

Titania

How do determine warmth and cold by colors,
What if red was icy cold and blue was burning hot?
Why are you so adamant with pre conclusions,
Why do you feel that everything in this world
Has aimed at only breaking you?
If I could tell you about the million times,
I was struck by something that I thought
Was coming to meet me,
Should I believe that everything out there,
Only wants to strike me?
But I have lived,
Countless number of times without being hit.
Only to learn that,
I should be prepared,
Perhaps for anything.

Caliban

If you feel without a purpose,
Do not despair.
We all were born as a part of a bigger play.
You do not have to be great,
Or achieve the stars-like success.
Just discover the pleasures of life.
Your time is numbered,
Your life is too.
Do everything you wanted to,
Do the things you thought you couldn't.
Not to be remembered, not to live.
But to be a part of everything.

Umbriel

Everyone thinks that outer space is an oblivion,
But the life you live is the same.
You are unaware of the things around you,
So caught up with trivial matters,
You forget that there exists a world outside too.
You think that everything outside your world only floats,
Bold of you to make assumptions.
At least we don't float in a world of lies.

Oberon

I have watched countless stars,
Yet none sparkle like your eyes.
I see the beauty of the universe in you,
Yet you still feel so shy.
I hope you destroy the word 'perfect'
Because not everything was created to perfection.
I wish you engulf every small flaw,
Because you are better than everything I saw.

Miranda

How bizarre it is, that you think beauty is flawless,
And that you believe everything in the universe is strikingly perfect.
But, look at me.
I do not look ordinary,
I am smoothly scarred on my surface,
Deeply blue within.
I am so unappealing that you named me after a monster.
But I have to tell you what I have seen,
This universe thrives in shades of different colour.
We're all out in some kind of space,
Just floating.
I wish your perception of me hadn't diminished my heart.
Scars, moles and freckles,
Birthmarks, tattoos, bruises all speckle.
They show you my journey and what I have been through.
No matter what you name me,
I am still a part.
And someday these scars are what I will be known for.

Ophelia

I think about the people who first discovered me
I know they don't exist
But if I could find out what they thought about me,
I wish I could see their reactions,
Or maybe the excitement of finding something new.
If only I could tell you how our first meet made me feel,
Stars exploded when I first saw you,
And in the storm, I floated casually.

Cressida

Lingering false hopes,

They stain my memories.

I knew you were wrong,

Yet I thought you would change

Like lyrics in a song.

But now that it's all gone,

I was told that we shouldn't travel paths

That hold dead ends,

But what do I do about crossroads then?

Daphnis

As we move farther from the sun,
Our planets become our world.
As we see the gases churn within them,
We wonder what life would look within them.
For now, we simply observe,
The movement of storms and the movement of us.
Only if we could see the treasuries that others held,
Maybe we would also scavenge.

Setebos

Once upon a time, stories scared me,
They start hopeful but they are pure horror stories.
You are mistaken if you think they have happy endings,
For no one tells you the tale after the end,
As then the whole story will seem like a lie.
Maybe that's why we can't relate to fairytales,
As the hero and villain, all look the same.
You think there is someone out there to save you,
From the clutches of evil,
But you have to do a lot of the saving by yourself.
In this process, victory is not what you will receive,
But it is self-discovery.

Mab

I have pale eyes as I have seen the world
In all shades of grey.
I realized people can be strange,
To reason for why they mend their ways.
Hopefully, you don't prove me right,
As I can tell by the eyes.
Cruel intentions are painted in those eyes,
And it all begins with a lie.

Cupid

I found out bullets fired in space never stop.
They travel in this expanding universe,
Until met by another crate.
You think the universe outside can be confined,
That somewhere there must be an end.
I like to think that our universe,
Is surrounded by black holes at each end.
They could lead somewhere else,
Or bring you back to the same place.
Your love might perish,
But mine will continue to travel like this bullet.

VI.

The Moon of the Earth

The Phases

We all reveal ourselves in phases,
Maybe that's why we hide in different places.
But the phases of the moon are different,
They harbor the night,
And their change does not make them glow less.
Only if you could reveal the masked,
Everything would not feel less.
As the month progresses,
I ponder at the phase,
Is someone out there actually seeing the full face?

New Moon

There are days I disappear,
For my phases demand me to go through light and dark.
As a free spirit, you search for me on days I am gone,
But forget about me as soon as I am found.
I have no dark story, no secret.
I represent fresh start,
For bad days don't exist every day.
So on the day I am gone,
Look at the empty sky,
And tell me what you wish to change.

The Same Moon

Ever wondered, why are you so fascinated by me?
It is only because I remind you,
What it feels like to be touched by the sun yet hugged by the stars,
To feel full and empty at the same time,
To be so near yet unreachable.
So there is one more thing I will tell you,
Just like me, you will always be in the right place.

Blue moon

They say patterns are established,
Routines are created,
Fate has already been written.
They tell you not to try,
Not to despair and not to cry.
But I am here to tell you,
Everything falls in place,
Dreams revive,
Eyes that once cried will smile.
After all the moon turns blue,
Once in a while.

Wolf Moon

The only animal that cries when it sees me,
For we have a love that no one understands.
I let them know where the others are,
And it cries for me, for we will never be able to be close.
But never does love falter for me.
Unlike you,
Once you find your special
You have forgotten me.
Why do you make the moon special,
Only when you miss someone?
Look at the wolf,
It loves me despite the clouds.

Bloodmoon

Habitual rituals that you think are divine,
There comes a night when even I glow like blood.
For the most atrocities that take place at night,
I am the silent observer until this night.
For on this night, I let the tides rise,
And befall anyone who causes harm.
Don't think no one is watching,
We are just silently counting.

The Side You Don't See

We all have two sides,
The yin and yang,
The day and night,
The dark and bright.
Just like how you know about the side you hide,
I hide the other side of me too.
We both hide our sides for the same reason,
We are unknown to how the world might react,
If they found out about what we truly are.

The Ocean

Me and the ocean have a beautiful bond.
I influence her every time I am near.
They say her tides are because of me,
But I am stopping her from being unleashed.
The ocean is extremely wild
And somehow I tame her.
But this isn't ideal in every case,
They say love isn't supposed to be tamed,
To which I fully agree.
But just as polar opposites,
I have to be her muse in every degree.

Super moon

Super moon is my favorite,
As that is the closest I will ever feel.
While everyone is busy capturing you,
I lie on my terrace just to gaze.
As huge and round you appear,
The more I feel I can see those craters.
Unafraid of what you have,
You flood the streets.
Maybe that's why they call you Super Moon.

The Star Pact

The stars are moon's friends,
Never do they overpower each other,
But all they do is compliment.
You think they make the sky look beautiful,
How do I tell you that without darkness they wouldn't?
So if you feel everything around you is dark,
Look again forgetful one.
Maybe you are the moon.
Don't search for your stars but search for your soul,
Stars will always linger next to you.

Eclipse

The sun and I have a friendship like no other,
And sometimes when I miss him,
We catch up.
It doesn't happen a lot but when it does,
Your world finds shelter.
For you believe that our power is the strongest,
And we may be what causes damage.
But I have to tell you,
For the short time, it happens,
We discuss about everything far stretched.
He tells me about the time he flared
And I tell him about the times I hid.
And like everything else we can't meet for long,
So we depart.
But we hope to see each other soon again,
In this lonely universe, he is my best friend.